WILD BABIES

Books written and illustrated
by IRENE BRADY

America's Horses and Ponies

A Mouse Named Mus

Beaver Year

Wild Mouse

Doodlebug

Elephants on the Beach

Wild Babies

Owlet, the Great Horned Owl

Books illustrated by
by IRENE BRADY

Five Fat Racoons by Berniece Freschet

Forest Log by James Newton

Have You Ever Heard of a Kangaroo Bird by Barbara Brenner

Animal Baby-sitters by Frances Zweifel

Rajpur, Last of the Bengal Tigers by Robert McClung

Gorilla by Robert McClung

Peeping in the Shell by Faith McNulty

Whitetail by Robert McClung

WILD BABIES
A Canyon Sketchbook

Written and Illustrated by Irene Brady

Nature Works
PO Box 360
Talent, OR 97540
(503) 535-3189
2nd Printing 1989
ISBN 0-915965-03-8

The following people made this impossible book possible:

Dave and Judy Siddon, who run a remarkable wildlife rehabilitation center near Grants Pass, Oregon

Laurie Marker and Capri Franklin from the clinic at World Wildlife Safari in Winston, Oregon

Dr. Steve Cross, Department of Biology, Southern Oregon State College, Ashland, Oregon

Mark Swisher, Scott Saul, Leslie Nelson, Ellen McMahon, and the other students of Southern Oregon State College who participated in the 1976 survey of bat populations of southern Oregon.

With their help I was able to observe, photograph, and sketch the baby and adult animals that appear in this book. Without their help, I could not have even begun.

Library of Congress Cataloging in Publication Data

Brady, Irene.
   Wild babies, a canyon sketchbook.

   Includes index.
   Summary: Bobcat and squirrel kittens, bear cubs, and other wild animal babies learn to survive in their canyon environment.
   1. Animals, Infancy of—Juvenile literature.
2. Parental behavior in animals—Juvenile literature. [1. Animals—Infancy. 2. Parental behavior in animals] I. Title.
QL763.B6   599'.039   79-12655
ISBN 0-915965-03-8

Author's Note

Western canyons take many forms. Some are steep and bare with rivers carving out mighty sculptures at their bases. Some are hot and dry, covered with cactus and sagebrush and rock slides. And some are gently sloping, with trees climbing their sides and bushes and grassy meadows softening the rough outlines. The canyon in this book is one of these—protected and sun-warmed on wintry days, and a cool place to sketch or lie back and listen to forest sounds on a hot summer day. A canyon like this offers many sorts of homes for different animals—caves, trees, bushes, meadows. It has enough water to keep it green but not enough to wash it away and the many kinds of food that different animals need to live all year in the same place.

I have learned to sit quietly and wait, and I have seen many small miracles. Bats swooping and drinking from a silent pool. Marmots sunbathing only a few feet from me. An owl that dives to answer a mousey squeak. A pine marten trotting along, sniffing at every drift of leaves or tangle of branches along its way. And yes, red-tail hawks mating in the bright spring sky and a tiny black-tail fawn suckling eagerly, its tiny tail whipping and flipping.

To see a wild baby is a miracle indeed, for wild mothers hide their babies. It is a very rare and special occasion when a human sees a newborn bear cub or bobcat kitten in the wild with its mother. A wild animal whose den or nest is disturbed will sometimes abandon her little ones, or in her distress and fright lose or misplace a baby.

For this reason, I did not try to find wild mothers and their dens or nests for this book. Instead, I sketched orphan fawns, cubs, kittens, and chicks as they were growing up at special animal care centers. Their nests had been destroyed or their mothers killed by accident, and the tiny orphans were cared for and taught to find their own food in the forest. Then they were returned to the wild.

Many people have written about the lives and habits of the animals in this book. From their experiences and from my own sketches and notes, these stories grew. And they are as real and as truthful as I know how to make them.

Wild animals are not good pets. As babies they may be cute, but they grow up very quickly and a home or back yard is no place for a grown-up wild animal.

If you ever find a nest of wild babies, remember that their mother may be watching you from a nearby hiding place, trembling with fear that you will kill or steal her babies. If you *truly* love animals and wild nature, you will creep silently away with empty hands and a memory overflowing with fuzzy little wild babies growing up with their wild mother the way they should.

Contents

Bobcat Habitat

It was early spring in the canyon when the mother bobcat sensed it was time for her kittens to be born. On silent feet she crept into the deep den in the rocks. As the full moon slipped up over the canyon rim, the muffled squeals of three newborn bobcat kittens joined the flutter and squeaks of the big-eared bats that hung from the ceiling high in the den.

The kittens were fuzzy with needle-sharp claws. They were only about five inches long. They could mew and nurse but their eyes were closed tight. The bobcat mother licked them dry and clean, then she stretched out on her side so that her kittens could find her nipples and drink their fill of warm bobcat milk.

2

The newborn bobcat kittens were pale pink, with gray spots on their white bellies and gray stripes on their faces. On their ears were tiny gray tufts and their tails were striped with gray. As the kittens grew older, these spots and stripes would turn a deep sooty black. Every kitten had a different pattern of spots and stripes.

When the kittens were about nine days old, their eyes started to open, first one eye, then the other, a little bit at a time. It took two days for this to happen. But even then they couldn't really see. Everything was out of focus and blurred. The kittens were cross-eyed.

By the time the kittens were two weeks old, their eyes uncrossed and they began to notice each other. Already their spots were darker, and now their personalities began to show. One was very curious. Another was shy and fearful. The third just wanted to sleep.

They started to wrestle and play when they were eighteen days old. Because of their sharp teeth and claws, their games often ended with scratched noses and flying fur.

Like all cats, bobcats have claws that can be pulled out of sight when they are not needed. This keeps them from catching on things when they are walking.

4

Every battle and scuffle taught them how to use their teeth and claws, how to jump and roll, and how to keep from getting hurt. They would need to know these things when their mother led them out of the den into the woods.

When they were three weeks old, their mother brought them feathers and pieces of fur to play with, and rabbit legs to chew on. Although they stayed in the den, there were lessons to be learned from stalking a wasp or trying to climb up the steep stone walls after the bats far above.

A newborn bobcat has no need for eyes or ears. So its eyes are closed and its ears are small. But the kitten does need whiskers to feel its way in the dark den, so the whiskers are long and strong. A grownup bobcat hunts at night, and needs large ears for hearing sounds in the dark. By the time the kitten is two weeks old, its ears are about five times as large as they were when it was born. When the bobcat is ten weeks old, its ears are truly giant — about thirty times as big as they were at birth.

The mother bobcat often sat on a rock above a meadow and listened for mouse sounds. When she heard them, she would leap down upon the spot with all four feet, then slowly lift each paw until it uncovered the mouse. Then, of course, she would eat it.

6

She led her kittens from the den when they were about two months old. The kittens copied everything their mother did, and when they were nine weeks old, one kitten caught a careless sparrow. Soon they were all catching small things to eat.

If the bobcat were the same size as a house cat, its feet would look many sizes too large. But with such huge paws, the bobcat can spread its claws nearly five inches wide to grab its prey.

By the end of summer, the bobcat kittens were half grown. They had learned many lessons about stalking and hiding. They knew when to attack and when to run. They watched carefully for sick or injured animals that they might catch easily. They were finding nearly all of their own food. Two of the kittens stayed with their mother that winter, but one night when the snow lay blue in the moonlight, the boldest kitten leaped away in pursuit of a rabbit. When it had finished its meal and washed its soft spotted coat, it trotted on again, alone.

Squirrel Habitat

It was late winter when the young gray squirrel first felt the stirrings of motherhood. She scurried from tree to tree, looking for just the right hole. This canyon forest had many old oak trees with woodpecker holes and natural cavities where limbs had rotted away. In forests where there are few holes, squirrels must make their nests out of twigs gathered into a big untidy ball out on a limb. The squirrel soon found the perfect hole. She made it larger and lined it with a soft bed of shredded bark for her babies. Then, as squirrels often do, she prepared a second nest in a nearby tree.

The four squirrel kittens were born on the first of March. They were only four inches long from their noses to the tips of their long tails. Their eyes were sealed and the tops of their ears were folded down over their earholes.

Squirrels usually have fleas, and sometimes a mother squirrel moves her kittens to escape them. If one nest is disturbed, she may carry her kittens to the other. Sometimes she is careless and tries to carry one by the leg or head, but usually she grabs it by the stomach, which is the best place. Then the kitten curls up around her neck like a rubbery red collar, safe from scratchy twigs and rough branches during the journey.

When the kittens were a week old, they still had no fur. But their ears had unfolded and whiskers had sprouted on their muzzles. Now they could feel their way around in the nest. And they could squeal loudly if they were cold or hungry, or if a flea bit them.

On the seventh day, a weasel hearing a kitten squeal poked its long yellow head into the nest hole looking for an easy dinner. With a chatter of fright and rage, the mother squirrel leaped to the opening and left a long bloody gash on the weasel's nose with her sharp orange teeth. The weasel had barely tumbled out of the hole and down the tree before the mother squirrel had grabbed a kitten and started off to her second nest.

At five weeks, the squirrel kittens were almost too big for their nest. They wrestled and scrambled up and down the nest wall, napped, nursed, and bravely peeked out the hole. They nibbled on everything they could — the edges of the nest, the shredded bark lining, and each other. Sometimes the noise and action got to be too much for the mother squirrel, and she would slip out of the nest for a nap.

The kittens were almost two months old when their mother led them out of the nest for their first real look at the leafy world in the tree. That day and for the next week they stayed very close to the safety of the nest hole. They tried to eat everything they saw and soon they knew what was good to eat and what wasn't. They learned to climb and leap, to keep their balance and to watch for danger. Their mother always stayed nearby to protect them.

front foot

The feet of the gray squirrel are made for climbing and leaping. Soft pads, sharp nails, and long toes cling to bark. The gray squirrel has no thumb on its front foot.

back foot

13

Soon the young squirrels became bolder. They wandered farther from their mother each day. They made crooked stick nests and napped on them. Each day they practiced their jumping skills, using their tails like rudders for balance. On cool nights they wrapped their tails around their bodies to keep warm. They still came back often to touch noses with their mother, but they stopped nursing at eleven weeks. In June when their mother began to prepare for her summer litter of kittens, she chased her winter kittens away and built a cool summer nest out of sticks and leaves.

By the time winter came, the young squirrels were nearly full-grown. They knew how to find food, how to build a nest, how to watch for danger, and other things a squirrel must know to stay alive. A squirrel can live for fifteen years if it is lucky. It was a hard winter that year, but gray squirrels have keen noses and can smell a nut buried under six inches of snow. When the snow melted in the spring, there were many little round holes where acorns had been dug up.

But the squirrels missed a few and from these acorns tiny oak trees sprouted and climbed up toward the sun.

Bat Habitat

From the ceiling of a cave in the canyon rim, a colony of big-eared bats hung by their toes. Where they were clustered, the cave was only a narrow slit. But it widened out below to make a dark den for the old mother bobcat and her young. It was mid-June when the female bats gathered in the slit to have their babies. They swung their ears backward and forward nervously as the six-week-old bobcat kittens wrestled and growled and chased feathers far below. For one of the bat mothers, it was almost time.

Reaching up with the thumbs on the front edges of her wings, she hooked them into the rough stone ceiling. Now her body was in the shape of a cup, with all ten toes and both thumbs holding tight.

The tiny, hairless batling was born into the cup, and she leaned forward and licked him dry.

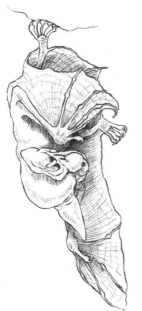

Then the batling found a nipple and clung to it with his mouth. His thumbs dug deeply into her fur. The mother bat slowly swung back down to hang by just her hind feet. The batling's hind feet crept upward until he could hook his sharp toe-nails into a crack in the ceiling close beside her.

He was several hours old when she left him to fly out into the dusk to catch insects. He tried to reach out for her and one foot slipped from the stone ceiling. For a few seconds he hung by five toes, squeaking with fright as he twisted and turned. But he found the crack again and hung on. If he had fallen, the bobcat kittens would have eaten him.

His mother returned
to the cave and squeaked
loudly for her baby. When
he answered, she lit beside
him and wrapped a wing around
him to warm him. A cave is a
cold home for a hairless batling
and he was very small — only two inches
from the end of his nose to the tip of
his tail. The skin that stretched between his fingers to make wings and between
his legs to connect them with his tail was velvety,
thin, and wrinkled. His ears were soft and floppy,
not firm and alert like his mother's. When he hung beside her, her nipple was in just
the right place for him to reach out and nurse. As she cuddled and licked him, he
drank the warm, sweet milk and then went to sleep.

When the batling was eight days old he fell, fluttering and squeaking, to the floor of the bobcat den. The kittens were asleep and their mother was out hunting when it happened.

The mother bat swiftly zigzagged down to rescue her squeaking baby. As the kittens crept closer, the mother bat spread her wings like an umbrella over her baby. The batling grabbed her nipple in his mouth and clutched her fur with his thumbs and toes. Then she flapped to the top of the cave with her heavy baby. The kittens meowed loudly, but the bats would not come back to be eaten.

This Myotis bat has much smaller ears and a prettier face than the big-eared bat. Other bats may have spots, strange flaps on their faces, no tails, or other interesting shapes or habits. Many bats eat only insects while others eat pollen or fish.

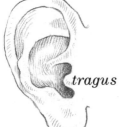

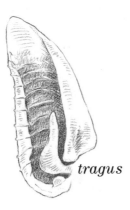

Bats are not blind, but their eyes are small. Since they fly at night and catch insects in the dark, they need more than eyes to help them. A bat's ears help keep the bat from bumping into things in the dark. As it flies, it squeaks loudly and steadily. The squeaks are too high for human ears to hear. When the squeaks hit something, the sound bounces back to the bat's ears like an echo and the bat knows where to fly to catch the insect or to avoid the branch or cliff the echo bounces off. This is called echolocation.

A human ear is stiff and thick. It can't turn to pick up sounds behind or in front of it.

The ear of the big-eared bat is thin and can move in any direction. A long, flat piece in front of the ear, the tragus, *vibrates when sound hits it and helps the bat to hear. A human ear has a tragus, but it seems to be useless.*

When a bat sleeps, it folds its ears back in a tight curl to keep them warm.

A big-eared batling grows very fast. It must be able to fly before it is a month old so that it can practice in the cave before going out in the summer nights to catch its own food. When it is seven weeks old it is chasing moths through the sky, and when it is two months old, its mother will no longer let it nurse.

When they were about eighteen days old, the young batlings began to try their wings. They spent long minutes opening and closing them in the dim cave. Then one would flutter down a few feet, catch itself in midair and flap its way back up to the cluster of bats. When the baby bats flew for the first time, they had to learn all at once how to use their wings and also how to listen for things that they might bump into. If they had landed on the ground, they might have been eaten by other animals or unable to get back up into the air.

As August with its hot days and short nights passed, the young big-eared bat began to learn the lessons he must know. He couldn't land on the bank of a pond to drink. A weasel or raccoon could catch him easily on the ground. He learned instead to fly low over a smooth stretch of water, open his mouth, and scoop up a drink. Once he dipped too low and flipped into the water. But a bat's wings make good paddles and he beat his way to shore quickly and climbed up a tree to dry in safety before flying again.

Autumn was coming.
All of the bats must be fat enough to get through the winter. Some bats
go south when cold weather comes. Big-eared bats hibernate, coming
out on warm winter nights for a snack. The little big-eared bat was
very good by now at catching insects. Squeaking, he would follow the
echoes to his prey. Scooping it into the pocket of skin between his legs,
he would reach down while flying and eat it. The soft moth wings
drifted down like petals in the evening air. Let winter come. The big-
eared batling was ready.

Deer Habitat

The sun was already long up when its rays crept down over the rim of the canyon and began to light up a tiny green meadow along the gurgling creek. They warmed the smooth tan coat of the blacktail doe and lit up the white spots in the orange fur of her brand-new fawn. The doe nudged her fawn gently. It was time to move to a safer spot.

The fawn woke slowly, his eyes blinking in the bright sunshine. He bleated in fright as the shape beside him suddenly grew tall and huge. Then the wet warm tongue touched his face. Mother! He gathered his legs beneath him and tried to stand, swaying on his wobbly stilt legs. Staggering this way and that, he lurched underneath his mother for his breakfast. She licked him as he suckled from one of the four teats between her hind legs. With every lick she learned the smell of her baby better. Now she could find him in the woods if he were to wander away and get lost. The young fawn did not have a very strong smell, but he did have scent glands between his toes that left a faint fawn odor on every step of his track. All blacktail deer have scent glands to help them find each other in the forest and to leave messages for each other in mating season.

Until it is about three weeks old a blacktail fawn cannot keep up with its mother if she must run from danger. So while she moves through the forest eating, the fawn lies still in tall grass or under a bush. Since a fawn has very little odor, a bobcat or coyote may pass just a few feet away without smelling it. And if the fawn lies under a bush, its spots blend in with the shadows of the leaves and make it almost invisible. One day a pair of bear cubs played for an hour all around the blacktail fawn without noticing he was there. The fawn didn't move an inch the whole time. When his mother returned after the cubs had gone, he leaped up stiffly and snuggled hard against her.

A buck deer grows a new set of antlers each year. They start as velvety nubbins in May, and by September they are fully grown and the velvet peels off in strips. They use their antlers to fight other bucks in autumn during the mating season. When winter comes, the antlers drop off. Mice and woodrats find these fallen antlers and eat them for the calcium and other minerals in them. In the spring, the buck's forehead bulges again with a new set of antlers. A doe does not grow antlers.

When the fawn was seven weeks old, he and his mother joined a herd of other does and their fawns. The fawns played all day, leapfrogging and boxing with their tiny hoofs, chasing grasshoppers, squirrels, and each other. They grew strong and swift and learned the many things fawns must know to survive and grow.

BLACKTAIL DEER

MULE DEER

*Deer have several scent
glands: in front of the eyes,
between the toes on all four
hoofs, inside the hock of the
back leg and on the lower
outside of the back leg
(metatarsal scent gland).
They use the scent glands
to mark territory and to
find each other.*

BLACKTAIL DEER
Antlers: two forked prongs
Tail: upper side and tip black
Ears: medium large
Metatarsal Scent Gland: about 3 inches long

MULE DEER
Antlers: two forked prongs
Tail: white with black tip
Ears: very large and mulelike
Metatarsal Scent Gland: 4 to 5 inches long

WHITETAIL AND KEY DEER
Antlers: tines rise from one main branch
Tail: brown on top, white underside
Ears: small
Metatarsal Scent Gland: round, about 1 inch long

WHITETAIL DEER

KEY DEER

30

As autumn came, the white-spotted orange coats of the fawns were replaced by thick, warm gray winter coats. The older deer, too, grew warm gray coats. The fawn was three months old when his mother weaned him. He was already eating a lot of tender plants, leaves, and acorns, and now she butted him until he stopped trying to nurse. All of the deer were eating as much as they could. They must be fat for winter when most of the food would be under snow. As the oak leaves faded from red to tan, the canyon woods echoed with the clack of antlers as the bucks fought each other over the does. Mating season had begun.

Hawk Habitat

It was a cold and frosty March morning when the female red-tailed hawk laid her first egg in the old crow's nest in the top of the oak tree. All around her the canyon was cold and bare, windy in the open places and in her tree. But it was time to lay the eggs, so she did. Setting on her eggs like a chicken on its nest, the hawk stared through the bare oak limbs and waited. Her mate brought her things to eat — a squirrel, a mouse, a sparrow — and she sat and sat. For thirty days and thirty nights she waited.

It was the middle of April when she heard a muffled tapping and a tiny peep as her first egg began to hatch. She rose to her feet and peered down at it, cocking her head to listen. Then she sat carefully back down to keep it warm. The chick was cracking the eggshell from the inside with a special hard point on its beak called an *egg tooth*. After several hours of hard work, the egg split open and the damp chick spilled out. Now the egg tooth would shrivel away because it wasn't needed anymore. As the first chick dried off and her downy white feathers fluffed out, the chick in the second egg began to tap and cheep. When the male hawk came to the nest with a mouse for his mate, he heard the chicks and fluffed his feathers excitedly. Now he would hunt harder than ever, for he must feed his whole family while his mate kept the chicks warm for another week or two. A cold rain began to fall as she sat on the nest, but she spread her wings a little and the rain rolled off her feathers on all sides. Underneath her, the chicks stayed cozy and warm.

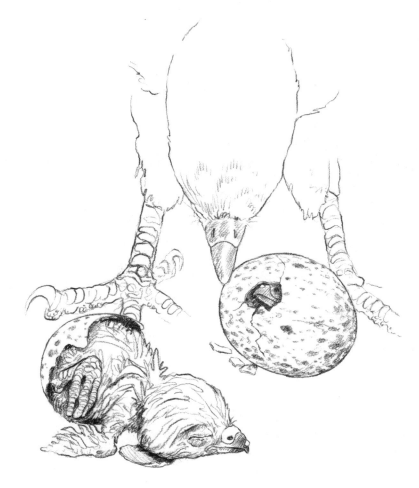

The chicks began to eat the day after they hatched. The female could squeak very loudly, and the male was a noisy little chick, too. Their mother tore the meat that her mate brought into tiny bits and offered it to the chicks until they could eat no more. She moved her feet carefully so that she wouldn't step on the young ones.

For the first two weeks, the chicks did not have much strength in their legs. They sat most of the time, squawking for food or grooming their pinfeathers, which got longer each day. Red-tail chicks are clean birds, and they always climbed up onto the edge of the nest to make messes over the side.

The chicks grew swiftly. Although they were still downy white, some adult feathers had started to come through on their wings and tails, and they were bigger than full-grown pigeons. They stalked around the nest, peering at bugs and moving leaves. Sometimes they stood and flapped their wings.

Only a week later, the chicks' white down was covered with new brown feathers except on their heads and necks, which were still downy white. They were seldom still, pouncing on sticks in the nest or hopping to nearby branches to explore.

When the sun was warm, they sprawled out in the nest with their feathers fluffed, soaking up sunshine.

By now, both of the
big red-tailed hawks
were having to hunt most
of the day to feed the hungry
chicks. Soaring above the oak
woodlands of the canyon, the
keen-eyed hawks would wait for a
flicker of movement in the grass.
Then, with a whistling dive and a thump,
they would have another meal for their
chicks. A young squirrel that wandered into
a grassy clearing made a good feed for the
squawking hawklets.

The chicks were seven weeks old when they began to feel a restless urge to leave the nest. At first, they flopped clumsily from branch to branch of the nest tree, stopping to scream for food when they got hungry. But soon they were making long jumps, and a morning came when one of them glided and flapped nearly twenty feet from a high branch in the oak to a low pine limb.

That was a turning point, and the two young hawks began to follow the older hawks, falling behind and resting, then trying again as the old hawks circled above them.

At nine weeks they were flying well, learning how to hover, turn, and land. As the spicy smell of hot pine needles rose in the air of the canyon, the four hawks rose with it, wheeling slowly, watching with sharp eyes for any small movement below that might mean food. The young hawks learned how and where to find and catch food by following their parents.

By now, the young red-tails were full-sized hawks. It would have been hard to tell the young birds from the older ones except that the adults had bright orange tails, while the tails of the big chicks were brown with black bars across them. The red-tail chicks would keep their dark tails until after their first molt during their second year.

When November snows blocked the ground squirrel and mouse holes, and many of the smaller animals that the hawks liked to eat went underground for the winter, the hawks had to soar farther and longer each day to get enough to eat. One cloudy winter day they stopped trying and flew farther south where it was warmer and more animals were out and around.

In the crisp air of March, the silence of the narrow canyon was pierced by a hoarse scream. Down in the oaks, a squirrel stiffened with fear — the red-tails were back! High above, tumbling through the air with flashing orange tails and white breasts, male and female red-tailed hawks were courting. They swooped and dove, clashing together with talons spread wide, then, releasing their hold, they soared apart. A hoarse scream once more floated in the air as the red-tails flew over their wild canyon, ready once more to begin a new red-tail family.

Bear Habitat

The mound of branches and tree trunks looked dead in the snowy blue shadows of the canyon. Nothing about it gave away its secret except a tiny wisp of steam that sometimes rose from the top. The snow around the heap of deadwood was deep and smooth. Who would have guessed that underneath was a hollowed-out space with a leafy bed — a warm, cozy den for a mother black bear and her fuzzy newborn cubs?

The bear cubs were born in the middle of February, and as soon as their mother had licked them warm and dry, they snuggled into the long black fur on her belly to stay warm and to nurse. The cubs were about five inches long, and except that they were much longer and had stubby tails, they looked very much like baby squirrels or baby mice. Of course, a baby squirrel's body is only two and a half inches long when it is born and a baby mouse will fit into a teaspoon.

If they were all the same size they would look like this

newborn   *newborn*   *newborn*
black bear   *squirrel*   *mouse*

For the first two months the bear cubs did nothing but sleep and nurse and sometimes squeal if their mother rolled onto them. They made a whiffling squeaking sound when they were nursing. Their mother was fast asleep most of the time. On a sunny winter day she might crawl sleepily from the den, eat a mouthful of snow and scratch for a while, but each time she came back to her tiny cubs, curled around them and went to sleep.

A bear doesn't truly hibernate — it awakens several times during the winter. But its breathing slows down during its deep sleep and it doesn't need to eat all winter. It stays alive on all the fat it stored in its body in the autumn.

By the time the cubs were two months old, they weighed about two pounds and were nearly twelve inches long. They were covered with coarse fur nearly an inch long. One of them was black like its mother, but the other was a bright reddish brown. Black bears come in all colors, from black to cinnamon to a yellowish cream.

In the middle of April, the mother bear woke up from her deep sleep. The sun was melting the snow and green shoots were poking up through the moist earth. The cubs followed her timidly from the black den, and for the first time they saw the canyon woods, warm with sunshine and noisy with courting birds. One of the first things the mother bear taught her cubs was to climb a tree when she growled a certain growl, for a tree is the safest place for a cub when a cougar or bobcat is passing by. And when one got into trouble she would march over and pick him up by the scruff of the neck and plunk him down where she could keep an eye on him. When she picked up a cub like that he kept perfectly still and didn't move until she put him down.

She taught them which green things were good to eat, and how to find grubs and insects. But the cubs were still nursing, and most of the time they just played, chasing through the bushes, wrestling and rolling on the ground — learning tricks of fighting and strengthening their muscles. Bear cubs don't make a sound when they play together. This is a good thing, for a tiny bear cub would make a fine meal for a hungry bobcat.

At four months, the cubs were full of mischief and curiosity. Sometimes they got a real surprise. A five-week-old bobcat is nothing to play around with!

In August the cubs were six months old. They were still nursing, but finding most of their food in the woods. Their mother taught them how to find wild bee honey. They stood up on their hind legs to reach the hive in the hollow tree. Bears do this easily, and can even walk around upright if they want to. The honey was so good that the cubs ignored the angry bees and were soon puffy from bee stings and covered with sticky honey and pine needles. It took all the rest of the day to clean up the mess.

As the days grew chilly, the bears ate and ate. They must get fat enough to go all winter without eating. They ate green plants and roots, blackberries and huckleberries. They ate insects and grubs, mice and squirrels when they could catch them. Soon they were tubby and waddled when they walked. One day the mother bear started behaving strangely. She poked under logs, prowled around fallen trees and stuck her nose into small caves in the canyon wall. Then she found what she was looking for. A tree had been uprooted in a wind and lay on its side. Where the roots had grown was now a big hole. Dead branches and bushes had covered the hole until only a tiny opening showed that there was a space underneath. When the snow started to fall, soft and deep, the old bear led her cubs to the tree, scraped open the entrance, and pushed them inside. Then she followed them and very carefully plugged the opening with dead leaves and sticks. The quiet snow drifted over their tracks and the door to their den, and when night fell their winter hiding place was safe.

Index